R0700701824 03/2023
**PALM BEACH COUNTY
LIBRARY SYSTEM**
**3650 Summit Boulevard
West Palm Beach, FL 33406-4198**

From the Train

Written by Megan Borgert-Spaniol

Illustrated by Rob Parkinson

GRL Consultant Diane Craig,
Certified Literacy Specialist

Lerner Publications ◆ Minneapolis

Note from a GRL Consultant
This Pull Ahead leveled book has been carefully designed for beginning readers. A team of guided reading literacy experts has reviewed and leveled the book to ensure readers pull ahead and experience success.

Copyright © 2023 by Lerner Publishing Group, Inc.

All rights reserved. International copyright secured. No part of this book may be reproduced, stored in a retrieval system, or transmitted in any form or by any means—electronic, mechanical, photocopying, recording, or otherwise—without the prior written permission of Lerner Publishing Group, Inc., except for the inclusion of brief quotations in an acknowledged review.

Lerner Publications
An imprint of Lerner Publishing Group, Inc.
241 First Avenue North
Minneapolis, MN 55401 USA

For reading levels and more information, look up this title at www.lernerbooks.com.

Main body text set in Mikado 24/41
Typeface provided by Hannes von Doehren.

The images in this book are used with the permission of: Rob Parkinson

Library of Congress Cataloging-in-Publication Data

Names: Borgert-Spaniol, Megan, 1989– author. | Parkinson, Rob, (Robert Anthony), 1971– illustrator.
Title: From the train / written by Megan Borgert-Spaniol ; illustrated by Rob Parkinson.
Description: Minneapolis : Lerner Publications, [2023] | Series: My world (Pull ahead readers. Fiction) | Includes index. | Audience: Ages 4–7. | Audience: Grades K–1. | Summary: "Linh sees many things while she rides on the train. Includes color illustrations and leveled text. Pairs with the nonfiction book I Ride"— Provided by publisher.
Identifiers: LCCN 2022008710 (print) | LCCN 2022008711 (ebook) | ISBN 9781728475936 (lib. bdg.) | ISBN 9781728478852 (pbk.) | ISBN 9781728483542 (eb pdf)
Subjects: LCSH: Readers (Primary) | LCGFT: Readers (Publications)
Classification: LCC PE1119.2 .B6734 2023 (print) | LCC PE1119.2 (ebook) | DDC 428.6/2—dc23/eng/20220310

LC record available at https://lccn.loc.gov/2022008710
LC ebook record available at https://lccn.loc.gov/2022008711

Manufactured in the United States of America
1 – CG – 12/15/22

Table of Contents

From the Train 4

Did You See It? 16

Index 16

From the Train

Linh sees cars from the train.

Linh sees homes from the train.

Linh sees art from the train.

Linh sees buildings from the train.

Linh sees people from the train.

What type of transportation do you use the most?

Did You See It?

art   cars   train

Index

art, 10   homes, 6

buildings, 12   people, 14

cars, 4   trees, 8